RAYMOND RABBIT
GOES
SHOPPING

Lynne Dennis

E. P. DUTTON · NEW YORK

First published in the United States 1988 by E. P. Dutton,
2 Park Avenue, New York, N.Y. 10016,
a division of NAL Penguin Inc.

Originally published 1987 by Macmillan Children's Books,
a division of Macmillan Publishers Limited,
London and Basingstoke, associated companies throughout the world

Typeset by Universe Typesetters Ltd
Printed in Hong Kong
ISBN: 0-525-44362-2
First American Edition   OBE   10 9 8 7 6 5 4 3 2 1

Raymond Rabbit
Goes Shopping

Raymond Rabbit and his
mommy were going
shopping. They made a list
before going out.
Mommy wrote:
     apples
     carrots
     purple thread
     light bulbs
     a new jacket
and — best of all — new
shoes for Raymond!

On the bus, Raymond
thought what color he
wanted his new shoes to be.

When they reached the
store, he and Mommy
carefully chose a shopping
cart that would steer straight.
Raymond also took a basket
for his new shoes.

Raymond Rabbit stayed
close to Mommy as she
chose big, juicy apples. He
saw pineapples, and thought
yellow shoes might be nice.

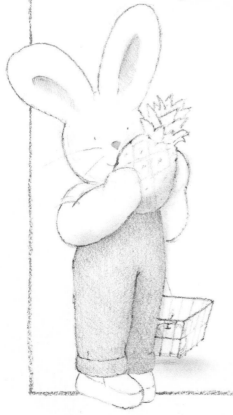

The carrots were on sale, so
Mommy bought extra.
Raymond nibbled on one
while he followed Mommy
around. Orange shoes would
be nice, too, thought
Raymond.

Next Mommy chose pink
yarn, but not purple thread.

She surprised him even
more when she put a brown
lamp in her cart and walked
straight past the jackets.

It was when Mommy admired a green dress that Raymond Rabbit knew something was wrong. Mommy never wore green dresses. Neither of them liked green. And this was not *his* mommy!

Raymond Rabbit ran as fast
as he could — right into
Mommy. She'd been looking
all over for Raymond and
was very happy to find him.

Raymond told her about the
pink yarn, the brown lamp,
and the green dress as
they walked to the shoe
department.

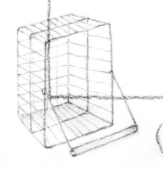

Raymond Rabbit chose red shoes — the same red as the dots on Mommy's dress.

Raymond and Mommy
started home. It had been
a long day. Mommy was
pleased with what she had
bought.

And Raymond really liked
his new shoes.